Butterfly Boy

by Virginia Kroll

Illustrated by Gerardo Suzán

Boyds Mills Press

Text copyright © 1997 by Virginia Kroll
Illustrations copyright © 1997 by Gerardo Suzán

Published by Caroline House
Boyds Mills Press, Inc.
A Highlights Company
815 Church Street
Honesdale, Pennsylvania 18431
Printed in Mexico

Publisher Cataloging-in-Publication Data
Kroll, Virginia.
    Butterfly boy / by Virginia Kroll ; illustrated by Gerardo Suzán.—1st ed.
[32]p. : col. ill. ; cm.
Summary : A boy and his grandfather joyfully watch a gathering of butterflies in
this story set in Mexico.
ISBN 1-56397-371-5
1. Butterflies—Fiction—Juvenile literature. 2. Mexico—Juvenile fiction.
[1. Butterflies—Fiction. 2. Mexico—Fiction.] I. Suzán, Gerardo, ill. II. Title.
    [E]-dc20   1997 AC CIP
Library of Congress Catalog Card Number 95-80778

First edition, 1997
Book designed by Tim Gillner
The text of this book is set in 16-point Palatino.
The illustrations are done in watercolors, acrylics, and salt.

10 9 8 7 6 5 4 3 2 1

For my son Joshua, with love
—V. L. K.

A niña cabeza de luna
—G. S.

E milio wheeled Abuelo, his grandfather, out into the sunshine, down the ramp that Papa had built.

"Wait for me here, and I'll get a book," Emilio said, darting back inside.

Mama and Papa said that Abuelo didn't understand words anymore, but Emilio was sure he saw a gleam in Abuelo's eyes whenever he read to him. He came back outside and pulled up a lawn chair next to Abuelo.

Suddenly Abuelo struggled to speak. He pointed with his good hand.

"Abuelo, what?" Emilio asked.

He followed Abuelo's eyes. Five crimson, brown, and white butterflies fluttered around the garage wall. They lit, fanned their wings, flitted about and landed anew.

"Butterflies," Emilio said. He watched Abuelo's face while Abuelo watched the butterflies. Emilio knew that Abuelo was smiling inside, even though his mouth could no longer show it.

Every sunny afternoon Emilio wheeled Abuelo out.
Together they watched the butterflies. After awhile,
Emilio got within inches of them. They let him stay
near as if they knew he would not harm them. Emilio's
next door neighbor, Mrs. Salazar, never called him by
his name after that. She called him Butterfly Boy.

When autumn came, the butterflies disappeared. Leaves of gold and brown and crimson fluttered in their place. When the weather grew colder, Emilio wheeled Abuelo to the window instead, and he watched swirling snowflakes turn the world white and hungry sparrows gobble the toast crusts that Emilio tossed to them each morning.

One day Emilio came home from the library and yelled, "Abuelo, look at this!" He opened a book about butterflies. "Remember our butterflies? They're called red admirals, and listen to this. They're attracted to bright white surfaces. They like to sun on them. That's why they're always on the garage, Abuelo, because it's white. They're hibernating now, but they'll be back in the spring and we can watch them again." Emilio saw Abuelo's eyes glisten as he stared at the pictures of the red admirals.

Spring blossomed, and Emilio told Abuelo,
"Not much longer."

One sweltering almost-summer afternoon, Emilio gazed out the window during math class. His eyes opened wide with wonder. Two red admirals fluttered through the playground and over the fence, toward Mrs. Cruz's petunias across the street.

Emilio squirmed like a caterpillar until the dismissal bell. He raced all the way home. "Abuelo!" he panted. "Guess what!"

He was going to tell him about the butterflies, but Abuelo began making sounds in his throat. "What, Abuelo?" Emilio asked.

Abuelo pointed with his good hand.

Emilio swallowed his words in a gasp. The garage was blue! Papa was painting it to match the house, which he had finished in the fall.

Emilio sped Abuelo down the ramp. "Papa!" he cried. "You can't!"

Papa's head jerked up. "Can't what?" His voice was sharp.

"Paint the garage blue. They won't come back, Papa. They only like bright white surfaces. Can't you change it back?" Emilio pleaded.

Papa took off his cap and wiped his brow. "Change it back? After painting all day?" Emilio saw frown lines on Papa's forehead as he replaced his cap and dipped his brush back into the can.

He also saw the clouds in Abuelo's eyes. Emilio's shoulders slumped. He watched five red admirals flitting here and there, turning circles. They reminded Emilio of wilting leaves tossed in wild directions by autumn winds.

Mama's laundry flapped gently on the line. Emilio watched as if he were in a trance. All at once, he leaped up. Two clothespins sprang apart and flew to the ground as Emilio grabbed his bright white shirt and scrambled to put it on. Then he stood, stiff and silent as a statue.

A minute passed. Fifteen minutes. Twenty. One red admiral fluttered close. Closer. It landed like a whisper on Emilio's shoulder. Soon there was one on his other shoulder. And another on his chest.

Mama came out to collect the laundry. She stood, gaping, as the basket tumbled from her hands.

Papa finished his last blue stroke. He took his cap off and wiped his brow.

Mrs. Salazar peered over her fence, clucking her tongue and shaking her head and wearing her broadest smile. "Incredible! Unbelievable, Butterfly Boy!"

Papa was startled. "What?" he said. Then he under-
stood.

Emilio heard Papa call to Mama, "I'll be home in
twenty minutes."

"Where are you going?" Mama asked.

Papa looked at Emilio and Abuelo as he answered
Mama's question. "To the hardware store for a few gal-
lons of white. Garage needs painting."

"Save some for my fence," Mrs. Salazar called. "It's
about time I painted it, too."

Emilio tried hard not to laugh. He felt as if his heart would burst from his chest. He kept his head still so the butterflies would stay, but shifted his eyes to see Abuelo's face.

The corners of Abuelo's mouth turned up, and his eyes danced and twinkled like twilight stars.